3 9082 11153 0492
First published in Great Britain in 1984
by Andersen Press Ltd.,
20 Vauxhall Bridge Road, London SW1V 2SA.
This paperback edition first published in 2008 by Andersen Press Ltd.
Published in Australia by Random House Australia Pty., Level 3,
100 Pacific Highway, North Sydney, NSW 2060.
Copyright © Tony Ross, 1984.

Colour separated in Switzerland by Photolitho AG, Zürich.
Printed and bound in Singapore by Tien Wah Press.

10   9   8   7   6   5   4   3   2   1

British Library Cataloguing in Publication Data available.

ISBN 978 1 84270 743 2

This book has been printed on acid-free paper.

TONY ROSS

I'M COMING TO GET YOU!

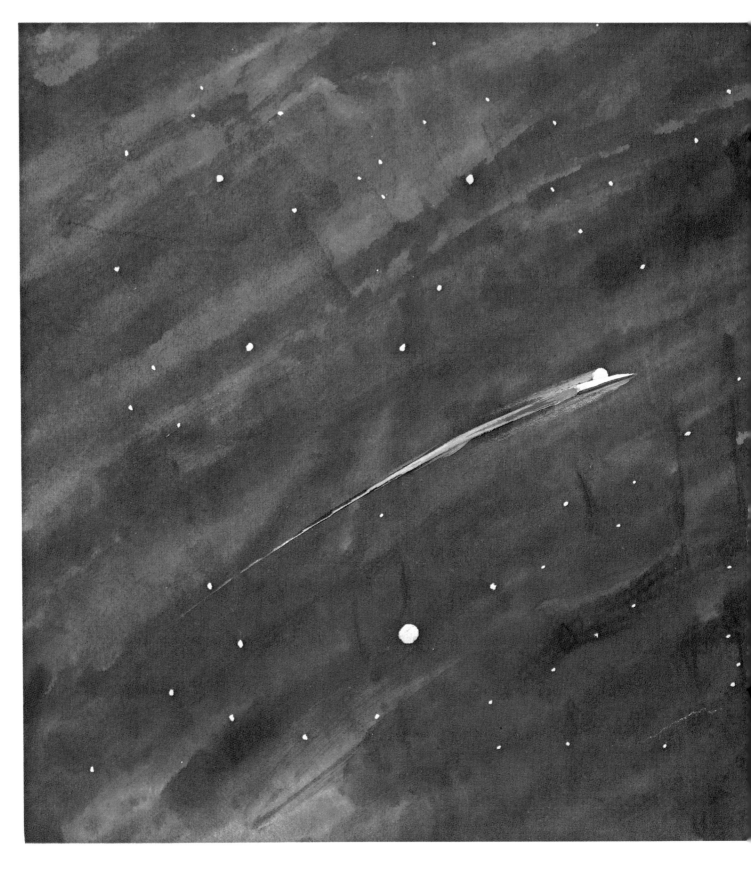

Deep in another galaxy, a spaceship rushed towards

. . . a tiny, peaceful planet.

It landed, and out jumped a loathsome monster.

"I'm coming to get you!" it howled.

The monster crushed all the gentle banana people.

It smashed their statues, and scattered their books.

It chewed up the mountains,

and drank the oceans. It had jellyfish for afters.

It gobbled up the whole planet, except for . . .

. . . the middle, which was too hot, and the ends, which were too cold.

Still hungry, the monster flew off in its spaceship, nibbling small stars on the way.

It had seen a pretty blue planet called Earth.

The monster found little Tommy Brown on its radar. "I'm coming to get you!" it roared.

It was bedtime, and Tommy was listening to a story all about scary monsters.

The spaceship neared Earth, and the monster found out where Tommy lived.

It circled the town, looking for the right house.

As Tommy crept up to bed, he checked every stair for monsters.

He looked in every place they could hide.

Once, he thought he heard a bump outside his window.

The monster hid behind a rock, and waited for the dawn.
"I'm coming to get you!" it hissed.

In the daylight, Tommy forgot all about monsters, and he set off happily for school . . .

. . . but then, with a terrible roar, the monster pounced!

OTHER BOOKS BY
TONY ROSS

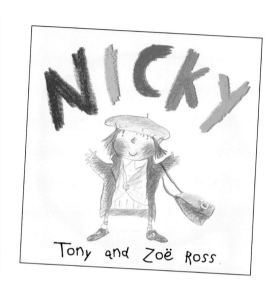

The Little Princess now stars in her own TV series!

Look out for all these titles at your local bookshop.